THE LIFEBOAT AND

OTHER SHORT STORIES.

BY KAMBIS RIAZY

(APEIRON KAMBYSES)

DEDICATED TO ALL

THE FREE SPIRITS

The Lifeboat   4

Beyond the Hills   22

The Drowned Colors   29

The Battlefields of the Naive   33

A Human Exhibition   38

The Comfort of Blood   47

The Limping God   57

The Dream Traders   68

The Ethics of a Genocide   74

Circus Maximus   82

The Dancing Ravens   93

Saint Sayyaf   99

The Reign of Darkness   106

The Reflections of a Judgment   112

The Lost Prayer   120

The Departed   126

The Unforgettable Wounds   134

Shades of Pain

139

The Fading Memories   147

The Tamed Souls   153

The Lifeboat

The giant city was grey and cold. Concrete and steel defined the soul of the entire city. The chilling wind helped the city to imitate the noises of vividness. It was the city, where eyes never met, hands never touched and love never existed. He was one of the millions that inhabited the city. Neither his work, nor the place he lived was spec⁻ tacular. His small apartment was on the twelfth floor of a tall building with large windows that faced busy, yet lifeless streets. The further away you looked out of those windows, the more con- crete you would find.

Every time before he turned his key in the keyhole to open the door, he knew exactly what image to expect; his beloved furniture in the dark living room. Without his noticing, his table and chairs had become more than simply the wooden equip- ment of a small apartment. They were rather like silent and static companions, always patiently lis- tening to his silence.

Days started and ended in a very similar manner. A quick cup of black coffee and a toast in the morning and a light dinner in front of his tv at night. The shows on tv portrayed what a set of apparently happy and successful people would look like. They all seemed to him to carry an invisible sign around their necks with huge letters that said : "I AM FAKE!", but he was usually too tired to care and merely sought to hear some human like voices with an occasional empty laughter. He spooned his food slowly and fed himself carefully, while pretending to enjoy the shows. This ceremony would repeat itself every night, until he would feel exhausted enough to enter the bed. After all, another long day awaited him tomorrow.

The first noise in the morning that encouraged him to leave the bed and to exist anew, was the piercing screams of his alarm clock. It would be 5:45 in the morning and darkness still dominant. He would press his eyelids a few times and jump out of the bed quickly towards the bathroom. Not even one single minute could be wasted. After a brief shower, he would brush his teeth and shave his face. It was necessary to look as closely as possible to the appearance that was considered civilized by the society.

The train that was meant to convey him and many others to their cherished destination appeared like a silver arrow dividing the dark tunnel into two halves. The crowd that anticipated this moment would rush into the train, so their daily routine wouldn't be delayed. All their faces were morbid and empty of any human emotions; even the most minute muscles were motionless, as if trained to respond to the dull ride that was only an introduction to an even more senseless day. Only the irregular shakes of the train managed to make the passengers appear alive. The fear of any possible eye contact with the others governed the silent atmosphere in the silver train. Some seemed to be mesmerized by numerous posters in the train that advertised products and services promising a happier existence. And others simply tried to look busy and not able to communicate. The crowd created the perfect impression of crammed cattle that silently accepted delivery to the next slaughterhouse.

At work a pile of paper was placed close to one of the outer edges of his desk. Different shades of yellow could be seen on the paper tower; the frail papery reminder of a colorful autumn foliage that had become a reflection of his own life. The daily greeting of the yellowish pile was a silent invitation to continue the work. Work that now could be done mechanically and without the need to think. The almighty system had replaced his mental sense of orientation long time ago. Daily routine defined all his actions and decisions. Luckily it was no longer required to act like a logical creature with all its human flaws. Being similar to a machine that followed exact instructions was desirably sufficient!

Without the necessity to check the time, he some⁻
how could sense when the breaks and the ends of
his shift were approaching. He usually would check
the large clock on the wall in front of him just to
confirm his feeling. Although there wasn't much to
look forward to in his apartment, he felt relived to
have survived another shift at work.

Usually when he reached his apartment, it was al⁻
ready dark outside. As always, he carried his din⁻
ner plate and placed himself comfortably in front
of the tv. Many nights he was too exhausted to distinguish any words and the voices that the tv produced became vicious and strange murmurs. On
the screen a small boat heaved gently, as if dancing freely atop the waves. The simple wooden
structure, which seemed to be the only authentic
and vivid part of the image, captured his attention
in an instant. It took him suddenly to another
world; he could imagine himself sitting in that tiny
boat and sailing through the wrath of the oceans
towards the unknown; free of all misery and sor-

row, only focused on a destination that didn't exist. Even the imagination of this endless freedom was breathtaking and the unique thrill unexpected. The fascination did not last very long, as a sudden loud noise that probably came from outside dragged him back to reality. Out of breath, he was still in his living room and some of his dinner was still in front of him. His first thought was how to get his imaginary boat back. The desire to own a raft that would set him free governed his mind. He stared at his greasy spoon for a brief moment and then softly started paddling with it in the air, in an attempt to revive the indescribable sensation. The oasis of his brief dream had to be recaptured and there was only one way to get there, by boat!

Next morning when the alarm clock warned him about the start of another day, he felt an unusual excitement within, for the fascinating impact of the boat was still alive. The liberating ferry's image was etched in his soul and he was not able of thinking about anything else. His movements were much slower and the fear of being late for work was fading. Even the daily shave was forgotten. It was the first time that he looked forward to the start of the day, as if he might get a bit closer to the boat of his dreams by the end of it.

The boat overshadowed all his impressions of his surroundings. The various patterns, he has been exposed to up until then, started to resemble boats or rafts. Even the silver train appeared like a giant metallic steamer, powerfully continuing its floating journey through the dark tunnels. A wide grin covered his face, as he was being shaken by the moving train. He was the only smiling passenger!

When he arrived at his office, nothing had changed except his attitude. The daily yellow wink of the paper pile was now transformed into merely another invisible feature of the dull office. As usual, he placed himself behind the desk with a quick heap. The passion to work had vanished, as did his ability to predict the time. Desire to be freed had replaced the urge of being productive. He then closed his eyes for a brief moment and all he could see was the precious wooden Redeemer that mesmerized him like a luring siren on trembling waters. He swiftly grabbed his pen and a piece of paper from the pile in front of him and without noticing started to draw. The lines and curves would not make any sense to untrained eyes, but he knew what the drawing was going to represent. The process of revitalizing his imagination in this unexpected manner was joyfully irresistible and he enjoyed being delivered to the powerful dream. Suddenly he was forced to return to reality by the cold voice of one of his colleagues who asked him about a project he was supposed to be working on. With a subtle sign of shame he quickly covered his drawing and tried to distract the coworker, while gently putting it in his pocket. His heart started to beat faster, as if he was about to be caught doing something illegal.

When he returned to his apartment and looked out of his windows, the concrete that surrounded him resembled an endless grey ocean that was waiting to be discovered; if only he had a boat! Driven by an unknown intuition, he reached deep in his pocket to fetch the piece of paper with the unfinished drawing. After a brief glance at the drawing, a wide grin covered his face. The unintelligible lines and curves seemed to have become an eternal source of inspiration. It was time to complete the drawing and bring his imagination to life. The night was going to end almost like all other previous ones; the tv made loud meaningless noises, he was placed comfortably in front of it, but the dinner plate and the greasy spoon were replaced by the unfinished drawing and a pencil. The hunger and the traces of the long day were softly disappearing.

The few lines on the yellowish piece of paper were about to give birth to a liberating idea. He jotted down with hasty motions any possible improvement, the necessary materials, and size and weight of the structure. Every added feature brought the boat one step away from his phantasy and closer to a tangible reality. Soon the details and information to improve his plans dominated most of the surface of the paper. The yellow piece of paper seemed to be infused with new life, which pushed all the previous data away. Captivated by his aspirations to complete his plan, he didn't even notice how long the process had taken. Suddenly the cries of the alarm clock that penetrated through the walls of his apartment brought an abrupt pause to the process. It took him a few moments to recognize the noise, he has been exposed to on a daily basis for so many years.

It was the early dawn, as he left his apartment to catch the silver train again. His passionate but exhausted red eyes made him stand out in the crowd. He was the only person that was not forced to be there. He felt like a newly liberated slave and was determined to celebrate his feeling. He got off the train a few station before his usual destination. As he left the station, the yellow piece of paper seemed to be his only real companion. He would stop every few minutes and have a concentrated look at the drawn desires and then with a reinforced smile he would continue. He felt, as if he was guided by an unknown force through the grey streets that didn't seem to have the oppressive impact they used to.

As he spotted the promising neon sign of a hardware store in the distant horizon, he knew he was getting one step closer to his promise land.

His first spontaneous decision brought him to an unknown place, where he was greeted by various new sensations. The warm fragrance of fresh timber, the jingle of metallic tools, the tingling excitement that dominated the air.

He felt like an insignificant particle lost in a jungle of the endless seeming rows of immense shelves. The joyful glint in his eyes indicated that he enjoyed getting lost among the metallic trees that carried the fruits of vast possibilities. The desire of breaking all the limitations set by time and space!

He left the store after some unknown time, pas‐ sionately holding a bag full of new ideas and fresh hope. It was amazing to realize how a small col‐ lection of wooden rubble could change his percep‐ tion towards everything; even the journey back home and opening the old door had become an ex‐ citing prelude to greater adventures.

Soon in his living room again, he prepared to begin realizing his dreams. He carefully placed the piece of paper on the table and spread all the wood on the floor in a way they would resemble the skele‐ ton of his boat.

The countless hours of passionately hammering now defined his entire day. Every once in a while he would stop the work and check the drawing to make sure that its promise was fulfilled.

The rudimentary workshop in the middle of his liv‐
ing room had become a haven. It was the hope of
reaching his destination soon that mesmerized
him.

The tranquility and flow of the work was inter‐
rupted at the dawn of the third day, as the phone
suddenly started to ring. He stared at the source
of the intolerable noise for a brief moment, but he
didn't have difficulty ignoring it. For the first time
he didn't sense the necessity to respond as there
were tasks of higher priority to attend. He could
imagine, who was on the other side of the phone
and what the message would be. The routine that
used to define his daily existence had been forgotten for now. But there was no regret; but he had
to finish the boat very soon. Without a pay
cheque, he wouldn't be able to afford more wood
to complete his boat, however had reached a
point, where resignation could not be an option,
the fight had to continue, the dream must be ma-
terialized.

On the next day, knowing that there was no other way out, he took all of his savings and headed to-wards the hardware store once again, being convinced that his calculations were reliable. He decided to buy as much wood as he could pay for; even the few coins he would receive in return, should quickly be invested in nails and other cheap tools. Total desperation was written all over his face, yet he had to fight on and build his life saving boat.

Days went on and his masterpiece started to take the shape of a real boat. He was hoping to accomplish his dream within the next few days, because his food supplies were getting very low.

Now that the time was against him, even the simplest motions were associated with excruciating pains. Days were long and fruitless and the boat still far from how it was meant to appear. He then stopped hammering and stared at the boat with its endless list of necessary improvements. The urge to stop the process immediately was overwhelming. A return to his previous life was still possible and the simple old routine seemed to be a reachable shore.

He slowly stood up, his breathing heavy and deep. The power of frustration was immense and intol‾erable. He dropped the hammer and started suddenly screaming and kicking against his own creation like a maniac. His cries could be heard miles away. He felt the total exhaustion in his even smallest muscle and bone. His shaking knees failed to carry his soul. His eyes were filled with tears and the last few kicks made even standing upright impossible. It was just a matter of seconds that his body would give in and he would collapse in the vicinity of the unfinished and now damaged boat. As he woke up hours later, it was getting dark out‾side. He then glanced at the remnants of his wooden companion, which was now the source of hope and sorrow simultaneously. He felt the renewed urge to complete the dream. He didn't have enough wood to repair the damages; he looked around and realized he was still surrounded by his beloved furniture, which now could serve him in a special way. The completion of the boat was the highest priority.

The disassembled chairs , the table even his bed and the noisy alarm clock soon became the indis⁻ pensable parts of the precious boat. He was now ready to be carried to his imaginary oasis.

The improvised shipyard with the completed raft in its center blew fresh life into his entire apart⁻ ment. It was time to break the invisible chains and sail away. His face was exhausted but carried at the same time unmistakable signs of relief. He was now a lot skinnier and had a long beard. He was still in his dark red pyjamas because he didn't feel the necessity to impress anyone anymore.

The last boundary on his way to the desired free⁻ dom was the thick window glass in front of him. He lifted his tv and used it like a battering ram to break through the glassy gates that held him back.

Pieces of shattered glass and bright sparkles from the tv filled the very silent soul of the night. He then sat in the boat and with the last bit of power pushed the raft towards the unknown paradise.

Beyond the Hills

The hasty return of a small boy, who seemed to escape from an unknown source of fear, didn't seem to bother the flow of the daily life in the village. The farmers and store owners simply continued their usual endeavours. All the noises of the lively village carried on without a slightest interruption.

Meanwhile the boy almost entirely covered with a thin layer of dust, kept running aimlessly through the crooked and narrow streets. His face was pale and lifeless, and although he had difficulty breathing, he seemed to be destined by an invisible force to continue his run.

Nobody noticed his quick and irregular steps, nor the traces of the sorrow on his dusty face. No one was interested in imagining what kind of nightmare he must have witnessed that encouraged him to escape. The wide open eyes frozen on his face made him appear, as if he was never capable of smiling. Only sharpened eyes would see his invisible tears and only sensitive ears could hear his inaudible screams.

He didn't know where he was heading; in an attempt to find a spot of tranquility, he continued his escape and increased his distance from the center of the village.

The shadows of a large tree seemed to be the only available refuge inviting him to rest. On his mind the images were still present and the scars still fresh. His sweat left tiny streams down his dusty face and found their way towards his neck. His breathing was still extraordinarily fast and not harmonic. Peace seemed to have vanished forever from his soul. The hope of retrieving his playful and passionate spirit and to forget the horrific images was an unreachable utopia. He stared at a point on the ground without being able to do anything else. He knew the horrific images would soon reappear, as if all of what happened would be forever rehearsed in front of his eyes. He pressed his eyes with his small palms to reduce the intensity and vividness of the images. But one by one the impressions would soon sneak through his shivering fingers and penetrate his brain. Sheer terror gripped his soul and would not let go.

The quiet hills, which were the furthest point known to him, isolated the village from the rest of the world. They appeared to be a perfectly deceiving playground. But the innocent playtime was not to last long. Sudden screeching cries drew his attention, and he began to crawl cautiously towards the source of the unpleasant sounds. At the top of the hill he stretched his neck to see beyond the hills.

A few young men dressed in military uniforms marched up and down, their mouths covered with foamy layers of wrath. Armed with swords, which reflected the sunshine in every direction, they would attack anybody; young, old, children, women. The soldiers kept swinging their mighty weapons and slaughtered any moving soul. A motivated and ruthless team of executioners searching everywhere to find more victims.

Meanwhile the severed heads and limbs created splashing fountains of blood that painted the entire scenery in an unusually saturated red. Blood was everywhere and the image was filled with screams and flames.

The small boy that was by fate to be only a passive observer of this great calamity felt determined to help somehow, but his limbs were hardened and immobile. Even screaming seemed to be an impossible undertaking. Sheer shock froze the boy in time and made him incapable of doing anything to challenge the misery.

Days have past, yet the haunting scene seems to have gained even more intensity. The detailed memories are still vivid and the many psychological wounds, the trauma left on his tender soul are noticeably painful. A strange medley of anger and guilt crushes him from within; the silent punishment for being an incapable observer watching the entire procedure from a safe distance. Although he knew he shouldn't consider himself accountable for the bloodshed, he still wished there had been something he could have done.

He felt his spirit was being buried underneath the dusty layers of agony of the heinous memories. A peculiar desire to return to the hills slowly over-whelmed him. He felt like a criminal, doomed to go back to the crime scene. Returning might not be the solution, but he was not able to withstand the urge that seemed to have taken control over his mind.

The second attempt to climb the hills was even more tiresome and energy consuming, than the first one, although everything about the route re-mained familiar. Every step was painful. Every breath whipped his soul anew, but he was driven to continue.

Out of breath, he finally reached the top. The spot where had lain last time revived all the memories.

He was not sure whether he would have courage to have another glance beyond the hills. His breathing was getting anxiously heavier and his heartbeat more intense. He pressed his forehead against the rim of the hill and could feel the heat the came off the sand and warmed his chest. The pressure to raise his neck was becoming more powerful than the fear. It was too late to regret and he needed to bring peace back into his exhausted soul. He took a deep breath and slowly raised his head.

The Drowned Colors

It was the last night of his performance. Just minutes before the start of the final show, a heavy rain had changed the entire image of the city. He could hear the cheer of the audience from the distance. It was only a matter of a few more minutes and he had to go through his old routine again; but the magic of being on stage was gone a long time ago and he didn't experience any sensation or excitement, as he used to. He stared at the mirror, as if trying to recognize the exhausted face that was buried under the heavy makeup. The joyful facade was perfect and ready to create some bursts of laughter. But his glance went deeper than all the colorful layers of his mask and see a different side of the showman. Just a few more minutes and his assistant would hastily enter the room and direct him to the darkened stage, a few more minutes and the waiting was over. He still could hear the rain droplets knocking on his window like a of thousand of impatient fingers. His quest was about to find a rest. Then the noise of somebody's unconsidered steps through the mud outside, forced him to return to reality. It must have been the assistant, he thought and sipped some water from the glass in front of the mirror. He closed his eyes and expected the opening of the door at any second. The steps had become slower and more muffled in the rain. He imagined raindrops swallowing any other sign of life; the hasty steps and the passionate roars of the crowd, all disappearing in one instant. It was all rain. At this moment he opened his eyes again.

The old man in the mirror was still there and patiently looking back at him with demanding eyes. A final decision had to come soon, but he was mesmerized by the impressive sounds of the almighty rain. He leaped up and with a sudden and uncoordinated move he approached his door. As he took about two steps outside the cabin, he heard the voice of his assistant claiming to have searched everywhere for him. These words were very familiar to his ears, although he wasn't able to detect any passion or vividness in them. He stood still and turned slowly around. The rain had started to wash some of his makeup away; his hair had become soft again and covered part of his forehead. He collected his breath and then with a rough voice yelled: " Your clown is finally dead!"

The Battlefields
of the Naive

"Fear not, for I am only your enemy! Our hostility and hatred are the strongest and most passionate human emotions. I don't know your name and don't understand your language and there is nothing I could associate with your face. But nevertheless, you are the enemy! The battle cries can be heard loud and clear, although their true sources are all far away from this hellish place. The leaders claim, it is our duty to feed these soulless grounds with our bloods and to wipe out the evil. Your existence merely gives a face to the unknown evil enemy. Without knowing why, I shall feel honoured to pull the trigger, for I am on a peace mission!"

And suddenly he found himself in a large hall, sur⁻rounded by people, he never had seen before. All of the unknown crowd, who were dressed in an almost royal attire, had one in common; they all seemed to be richer and more powerful than he could ever imagine to become.

A mesmerizingly huge and radiant chandelier hung from the ceiling, whose sheer size gave him the impression that it would tear down the entire building in any moment. As he walked towards the center of the glorious hall, he realized that the faces started to turn towards him. The admiration seemed endless; those that knew his story told it to others, so they all collectively could show their respect; the uncomfortable side of being the centre of attention was that he had to show to almost everybody subtle signs of his gratitude.

The crowd slowly started to gather themselves and became less talkative. Now he could even hear the soft crushing noise created by his shoes over the velvety red carpet. Although he wasn't sure whether he belonged there at all, he decided to continue the silent walk.

As he was approaching the centre of the hall, the crowd , while greeting his arrival with a unified cheer, divided itself to either sides to clear the way for the new hero. He raised his right arm, as a sign of respect to the spectators, but internally he felt like Moses performing a powerful and impressive miracle, dividing the human stream!

And then it was the king himself that was holding a cushion with a small medal on it. The metallic honour was almost as illuminant as the large chandelier and its dark red ribbon gave it an elated image. A truly mesmerizing object that could overshadow everything, even the presence of his majesty, the king!

Quietly and carefully he stretched his arm, as if trying to offer the king a handshake. He could imagine the softness of his majesty's white silk glove. And then he gently pressed the hand; there was a sudden bang that woke him and forced him to return to reality. The white tenderness turned to rigid and dusty trigger. The glorious hall was no more and the inhuman and ruthless desert instantly pushed the magnificent images away from his mind. The blood soaked body of the enemy's soldier lied in front of him like a forgotten sacrifice at the altar of his feet. On his chest, where the symbol of his bravery was meant to rest, was a fresh piece of the moist and soft brain of the enemy, which seemed to be hanging from a dark red stain of fresh blood; a medal that would stay on his mind for the rest of his life!

He then looked at his prey and thought "Who is going to recognize this silent face among a large pile? The pile of dead dreams and wasted lives. And now on either side of this war, the only light in the cities were from the blazing yellowish flames of burning buildings and the only signs of life were the screeching cries of the suffering. Duty calls, passion fades, logic not existing! Thousands have been killed, countless will follow! Beauty crumbles, souls crushed! In this human desert, only gods can laugh. May God save our king!"

A Human Exhibition

As the heavy fog of early morning started to disappear, sunlight encouraged the grey city to reawaken. The streets were about to be filled with daily life again, acting as the city's veins.

The central bus terminal of the town was populat- ed by a few passengers that were waiting eagerly for their bus. The waiting crowd silently attempt- ed to imitate the image of apparently successful individuals. They were unified by a passionate an- ticipation towards the journey that overwhelmed the atmosphere. Some of the passengers could not hide their excitement and stared frequently at the road, from which the precious bus was meant to come; as if their innocent and curious glances could cause its accelerated arrival. Others went through the catalogues or the maps they were provided with earlier and explained once more their expectations to their family members.

Suddenly a bus appeared on the distant horizon resembling a proud silver arrow, aiming the reflected sunlight towards its mesmerized audience. In a few moments the longed journey would begin and the hunger of the enthusiastic passengers would be satisfied. The approaching bus revealed more details of its fascination and encouraged the crowd to cheer its almost majestic arrival.

The chrome bus became then fully visible, floating in the midst of a dust cloud. The front door opened gently and a tall person stepped out of it with an elegant swiftness. A wide and somewhat sinister grin on his face, with a sharp and penetrating voice, he introduced himself as the tour guide and welcomed the valued passengers. After this short introduction and checking of tickets, the passengers were allowed one by one into the bus. To reduce the chances of any hazards at this early stage of the trip, the tour guide encouraged his excited clients to avoid a chaotic manner of entering the bus. A soft warmth greeted the people into the dimmed interior of the bus. The fragrance of a fresh spring breeze circulated throughout the bus, accompanied the initial pleasant view. The crowd tried to find the seats that were assigned to them on their tickets, which created a short lived chaos. The power of excitement was still dominating every aspect of the initial conversations. Some of the passengers checked the schedule once again, while others tried to get accustomed to the new comfortable environment. After the last passenger entered the bus and was guided to his designated seat, the tour guide reminded the passengers with a friendly tone to prepare their cameras and to sharpen all their senses. The carefully chosen words seemed to promise an unforgettable journey.

A dark tunnel not far away from the station conveyed the bus towards its cherished destination was perceived by a few as the first attraction of the journey.

Before the bus was about to reach the other end of the tunnel, the tour guide started to talk again. He warned his passengers that the journey would be a unique experience. The passengers would be taught new principles and values, which would dramatically modify the way they perceive their world. He reminded the passengers one more time to prepare their minds and cameras and to make sure not to miss even a single thing.

As the bus exited the tunnel and entered the day‐ light again, the tour guide said with a noticeable pride that the first event of the tour was about to reveal itself to the passengers. He asked the driver to go slow so that all the details would be ab‐ sorbed easily.

An old man lay in the muddy pedestrian zone. His underfed body was partially exposed to the hungry audience. He was shivering and showed no sign of power to move or even to keep his eyes open. He was holding a small paper bowl, although barely anything was in it. The spilled soup had created a brown puddle close to his poorly shaved face. The tour guide joyfully reminded everybody that they were witnessing genuine and authentic human suffering.

Suddenly one of the passengers, who was sipping his soft drink through a long straw, seemed to be very excited to see this event and intuitively opened his window. He apparently intended to take a picture of the old man from a shorter distance. As the tour guide suddenly noticed the open window, he rushed in one great leap towards the seat of the passenger and closed hastily the window. He then took a firm but still friendly tone in an attempt to justify his action, saying that it would not be recommended to let the unpleasant air of the outside enter the bus! These words of warning were then followed by a silent and affirmative smile and a penetrating glance at the other passengers.

The first sight promised to many a continuation of the entertainment and encouraged the passengers to look more carefully, so maybe they would be able to discover the next attraction of the tour. The dominating silence was then abruptly taken apart, as attentions were drawn to the other side of the bus.

A heavily armed soldier was pointing his mighty rifle against a small girl. The girl, barely reaching the height of the knees of the soldier, was holding tightly to a damaged doll in her right fist. The girl in her dirty tatters captured everyone's attention. The fear was clearly visible on her little face. Her loud and fearful screams penetrated through the thick windows and gently tickled the ears of her audience. The soldier in complete military gear stood like a strong and admirable hero in front of her and pressed the tip of the bayonet, which crowned his gun, against her cheek and seemed to prepare himself to pull the trigger. The soldier made sure to keep his distance, so his safety would not be affected and only the tip of his rifle would be soiled with fresh blood. But before this happened, the guide called the passengers to pay more attention to the next atrocity that could be enjoyed soon!

The guide said continued in a tone of pure astonishment that the passengers could thank god and consider themselves very lucky; it would not happen very often that so many authentic events could be seen in one tour. It was almost a miracle to find so much human misery on one day! He then pointed proudly towards the next attraction; in the middle of the road a middle aged man was setting himself on fire. As people saw this, they loudly started cheering from their comfortable seats. The bus then came to a tender stop in the vicinity of the fire. The crowd pushed at the windows that were closest to the blazing flames. Soon the man became a black pile of burnt flesh waiting to be tipped over very easily by the slightest breeze. The unforgettable end of a rebel!

The audience then turned to their guide in pure astonishment and speechless amusement, as if trying to thank him for unique experience. The guide replied with apparent pride and a gesture of satisfaction. He then nodded to the driver to signal the return.

The return trip was a lot more silent, the passengers were obviously impressed and entertained by the gloomy show of naked violence and bloodshed.

It was almost dark again, as the bus slipped into the terminal. The passengers collected their belongings and prepared to resume their stultifying routine.

 The guide smiled down on passengers and said :"Hope you enjoyed this trip and always remember life goes on, our life!"

The Comfort of Blood

Inspired by an Angel,

written by a Maniac

It was the third day after almost the entire village was burnt down by an unstoppable gang in filthy and tattered military uniforms. The members of the gang, mostly young men, who wore the exhausted faces of desperate peasants with countless scars, still patroled in the newly conquered village. Their muddy uniforms and rusty guns were intended to create a sensation of superiority and absolute power, although there was hardly anybody left to impress.

Three days had passed and only the sorrow was resurrected; nothing but the traces of the vicious destruction covered the meadow that used to be evergreen and full of hope and joy. The raging flames of the war were meant to be spread everywhere; no soul to be spared. A war, whose origin and cause still remained mysterious and

unimaginable, gave birth to more hatred and violence day by day.

The young soldiers on patrol sought out every neg-
ligibly small spot that could be used as a hideout.
"Traitors are like small worms and can hide in any
hole!" shouted one of the officers to encourage his
crew to search more carefully and not to miss a
spot. The heavily armed soldiers carried small
empty bottles fastened to their belts. The soldiers
protected these bottles, as if soon they would be
filled with means of divine invincibility.

A small stall,which was hidden by the shadow of
some large trees, drew the attention of a pa-
trolling soldier. The young soldier with an irresistible thirst for a heroic recognition by his comrades, prepared his rifle and made sure his small
bottle was still there, before stepping cautiously
into the small hut.

As he opened the door carefully, he was greeted
by pure darkness. He quickly swung his rifle to either side to show his eagerness to use it against

anybody hiding in the darkness. Suddenly the sound of an anxious breath, which came from one of darkest corners of the hut, captured his attention. With a loud bestial cry he demanded the hiding person step forward or he would open fire. Then before anyone could make any response, he ran towards the corner, where the breathing noises came from. In that moment he saw tiny feet suddenly appear in the river of light that found its way through the open door behind him. He unconsciously reduced his speed as in his mind the hiding person was transformed from a dangerous enemy to a potential prey. He threw out his left hand and grabbed violently at the tiny feet, while still holding his rifle in his right hand. He jerked the small body towards the stream o light, in an attempt to see more of booty. After making sure that the child was the only person in the hut, he reviewed instructions he had been given earlier by his masters. He was quickly convinced that his unexpected find rightfully belonged to him; a tribute to the glory of his patrol.

Suddenly the child started to scream and break into tears. The soldier released his rifle and si¯ lenced the child by pressing his muddy right hand over the child's mouth. With his left hand he started to undress the child violently The animalistic drive within the soldier alone dictated his behaviour. The enemy was completely personified in the little child, and it was his turn to take revenge and satisfy himself.

Afterwards the soldier straightened his uniform, jerked his bottle from his belt and pulled out a large knife from one of his pockets. He stared once more at the face of the child. Then he held his empty bottle close to child's neck and slowly pushed his large knife into a large vein. The child quickly showed less resistance and was soon motionless. The precious bottle soon filled with thick red liquid.

After a while the soldier left the hut, holding his rifle even closer to his heart than before. His uniform and his face were covered with a sticky mixture of blood, sweat and mud. His face emitted a peculiar medley of anger and relief. He tried to collects his thoughts, so he could melt again into the stream of his comrades. There was still a lot more to be discovered and much more blood needed to be looted, after all he had to please his masters and impress his fellow soldiers! Violence and brutality were the only moral known to the young soldier; they were not capable of even imagining another reality.

In the center of the village a vast tent was visible, where daily life used to occur. In front of the tent a large vessel was placed, flanked by the general and another person that resembled a successful and satisfied businessman. An old gramophone next to the vessel played a soothing old song, which entirely opposed the situation surrounding it. The ceremonial procedure was about to begin.

The soldiers built a well-organized queue in front of the tent and were holding their bottles with the collected blood. It was time to fill the large vessel.

While waiting in the line for their turn to pour their precious captured blood, some soldiers demonstrated proudly their bottles to each other. Many others seemed to be eager to empty theirs quickly and return to the battlefield to collect even more of the liquid treasures. Very few, if any, wandered, where the blood vessel would be transported and why it demanded their intense dedication.

As the vessel was almost full, the businessman signalled the general to halt the procedure to choose few reliable soldiers to guard the treasured vessel accompanying him. The general quickly complied and chose a few of his best soldiers. Among those soldiers, the young soldier with bloody stains from his vengeance against the small child, stood out.

The vessel represented hours of ambitious work and the death of hundreds and was to be conveyed as quickly as possible to its cherished destination, while its content was still warm and fresh. The young soldiers once again followed blindly the orders of his masters and simply did, what they were told to.

After a long journey through the areas that were hit by the misery of war, a castle that crowned the top of a green hill became slowly visible. It was placed at a safe distance from the rest of the world, so its inhabitants would not be annoyed by the uproar of the war.

The castle was of impressive dimensions; to evoke absolute dominance in every sense. The first thing to strike the eyes of any person entering, was the saturated red color of the walls and the furniture. It made the marble statues appear brighter; a mesmerizing combination of red and white.

While the soldiers were still realizing the details of the red chamber, the businessman ordered the soldiers in a sharp voice to bring the blood vessel to basement.

The basement was a moist and dim place and made even the seasoned soldiers uncomfortable. They placed the large vessel carefully on the ground and most were immediately ready to return to their familiar battlefields. But the young soldier is curiosity struck like lightning, and he looked around, trying to familiarize himself with the strange surroundings. There were other vessels that resembled the one that was just carried into the cellar and pieces of furniture that had strong similarities to those in the main hall. As he was about to join the others, a small stool captured his attention. The stool was half painted red and was placed close to another vessel full of blood. The captured blood was being used to produce the bright paint for the furniture.

The gruesome image created a maddening sensation in the young soldier, as realized for the first time what he and his comrades were fighting for.

An unintentional glance at his rusty rifle inspired him to a reaction; he swung the weapon to smash the nearest containers. Soon containers surrounding him were all shattered in pieces. Blood soon covered the biggest portion of the floor. Exhausted from his battle against the vessels, the young soldier was marooned in a red lake. He bent down slowly and dipped his fingers into the blood from the floor. He raised his blood drenched hand and stared at it. He then smeared his face with fresh blood, as if he wanted to be indistinguishable from the rest of the furniture and to demonstrate that he was of the same value; one of his masters' victory pieces!

The Limping God

The entire air was filled with a sweet smelling mixture of cheap perfumes. The squeaking sounds of an old gramophone lent the atmosphere an oriental undertone. The old bazaar was in motion with constant life. People in small groups walked up and down the alley in its middle. Some stopped for a while to sniff the fruits or to finger the carpets or just to have a deep and concentrated glance at other polished knickknacks. With their loud cries, the store owners tried to encourage the new visitors to buy something from their collection, as they promised the best price and quality in the entire city.

The overwhelming signs of livelihood seemed to melt all the present emotions and attitudes. Even the beggars were parts of this buzzing melting pot.

But in the midst of this chaos an old man, who had obvious difficulties in moving through the crowd, drew more attention. His heavy steps was inflicted with an agonizing limp. His old tatters were soiled by a dried medley of mud and his own urine, so that the odour overshadowed all the other smells in the lively market. He had a filthy and old patch over his right eye suggesting blindness in one eye. Attempting to increase his speed, which made his limping look even more severe and painful, he was determined to drag himself towards the center of the market. His face was focused and concentrated, as if he was about to convey an important message. While some people recognized his need and cleared the way, others still mesmerized by their surroundings, had to be pushed aside by the old man.

He finally stopped his painful journey in the midst of the market. He then cleared his voice and started to talk as loudly as he could. With an unpleasant yet powerful voice he recited some paragraphs from the Bible, which were meant to indicate the absolute superiority of his god. During this biblical presentation, he also demonstrated all of his rotten teeth and spread his foul breath. His image gave an impression of having just escaped from a mental asylum, where fed only by decomposing corpses.

His screams, however remained largely unattended by the busy crowd. In order to draw more attention, he changed his tone to a rougher and more penetrating level and said : "I am god the almighty himself. I have become flesh and have returned among you to give my precious human creation one more generous chance to be forgiven!" But his audience still did not show the response he was expecting; some people stared at him briefly, while many others ignored him and simply carried on their business. The newly declared god then challenged his audience and performed a mesmerizing miracle to prove his omnipotence.

Flashing lights and loud and hissing noises coming out of his pockets were created to impress the crowd. The entire market changed its attitude in an instance. The impact of this trick on some was visibly strong. Some followed blindly their instinct and approached this new god very cautiously. As god realized that at least a portion of the crowd was enjoying his show, he repeated his speech. He continued the show with some more sleight of hand. He obviously knew how to paralyze the spirits. He enjoyed the process of creating a new set of believers that soon could be transformed into his will-less army. Some members of the audience nodded to show their agreement and support to various of his statements. Their readiness to absorb the magic made god's performance even easier; they would tell stories from their own life, but they would try to tailor the stories to make them fit to the content of his speech. "He is the real god!" shouted somebody from the crowd and a few that were in the front row kneeled in front of the limping god. Soon others followed them and also kneeled, not only to show their total submission towards the newly discovered god, but also to remain valid members of the society. Soon a peculiar and impressive tranquility dominated. God was standing in the center of the market and many rows of the people kneeled around him. After a while a few persons that were obviously more curious than others raised their heads to risk another glance at their god. The second look at the god in their vicinity seemed to encourage the audience to remember all their complaints and their individual sorrow, which resulted in a chaotic human polyphony. Suddenly a person from the crowd tried to give the conversation a new direction and invited god to his house, so he could serve him with food, fresh cloths and any other earthly necessities. Before the old god could show any reaction to this passionate invitation, the same person continued, "the merciful god had taken a human shape, simply to show how close he really is to all of us. We are truly blessed! He has come as a human being and with all human needs and desires."

As soon as he finished this sentence, other people also showed their eagerness to invite god to their homes and receive some blessing as well. As they were waiting for an encouragement to demonstrate their desire to be closer and more pleasing to the god, a chaotic mixture of desperate joy and painful helplessness governed the atmosphere.

The old god stood quietly there, while he seemed to follow every slight development carefully. He was enjoying the quick progress of his divinity and a wide grin covered a great portion of his old and wrinkled face, as he was looking down on the loyal subjects of his creation.

By this time almost the entire present population of the market was conquered. There was barely any empty space among the excited crowd. They even pushed each other just to be a little closer to the divine beggar.

While the fatuous argument over hosting god continued, some people finally showed courage and approached god with various offerings; anything that was accessible to them at that moment that deserved to be considered a sacred sacrifice, fruits, live animals and fresh bread. The hungry god started immediately to devour hastily as much as he could. The mesmerizing fragrance of the fresh food drew also a few underfed children closer to the almighty. They surrounded him with the hope to witness his merciful side. Barely any of them was fully dressed, as if they were trying to proudly display their bony bodies to god and the rest of audience. The by now satisfied god held up a piece of bread close to the muddy noses of those children but unreachable by their small hands. It was an obvious attempt to tease his starving audience and to make his divine reign once more evident!

One of the suffering children, who was in the vicinity, observed him carefully. With the innocent curiosity of a child, he then asked the old man why he lacked any passion or power to change the situation and set an end to the misery of the living. The question did not to seem to please the merciful and loving god and with a voice filled with strong traces of hatred and revenge and a mouth full of half chewed food, he shouted, while releasing some of the precious food onto the front row of his audience, "Blasphemy! The child deserves the most severe form of punishment.", to which some of his believers replied with a quick sense of readiness to defend the honor of the almighty. They arrested the curious child, tied his hands and feet and started to whip him in front of the all powerful deity. Now god could enjoy the collective human agony once again.

While he continued to eat, he would encourage people to whip the child harder. The vicious whip easily tore through the skin of the child. His blood splashed everywhere and some streams of the red liquid even reached the cherished offerings in front of the god, which didn't seem to bother him at all. "Whip harder! You should whip his mouth too, where those filthy words came from. Let that be a lesson to the rest of the world."

The old god simply stood there and continued to eat the blood smeared offerings. After a while the child suddenly stopped lamenting. He didn't even move or show any reaction to his well deserved punishment! But his lifeless body was still being whipped to satisfy The Lord. After continuing the process of whipping for a while, one of the torturers approached the child to see whether the cheeky target was still alive. The child was entirely soaked in his own blood and barely resembled the curious child that stated his question moments ago. "He is dead. The enemy of The Lord almighty is at last defeated!", the torturer said with a proud voice. The audience, including the forgiving Heavenly Father, joyfully screamed to celebrate their unforgettable moment of victory and dominance. The vivid chaos was brought back to the old bazaar in a most glorious manner. Many of the be⁻

lieving mass would be encouraged to thank their god and to remember their day with a great pride!

The Dream Traders

Another day was about to begin, as the sun shone on the small village and birds of all kinds seemed to celebrate it altogether. The river flowed generously through the village and nurtured it like a loving mother that couldn't stand its thirst. All was peace and beauty in the purest and most complete form, it seemed.

The gentle jingle of heavy chains penetrated the thick walls of grey prison that stood in the center of the village. The preparation for the major event had demanded a long time; the gates wouldn't open for quite a while, although the readiness of people inside and outside the prison could be noticed easily. The noise inside the prison started to lose its initial intensity and piercing power and was audible only for the very patient and careful portion of the audience. The smell of excitement and enthusiasm filled the air in an instant.

On the other side of the square under the mighty shade of an old tree, on a soft and comfortable bench, a few persons were waiting and trying to entertain themselves with excessive amounts of colorful food and drinks that were spread before them. They all knew about this sacred day and prepared themselves accordingly.

The slow opening of the heavy gates, required a special ceremony by itself and tested the patience and tolerance of the attendants. The reunion of the people that were separated by the thick walls and the heavy gates was a matter of a few more moments.

In a despondent queue the prisoners appeared behind the open gate, carrying the heavy chains around their necks and ankles. A brown paste, a blend of their sweat and the dirty rust of the chains, covered most of the visible parts of their tired bodies and old clothes. They were encouraged to remain in their soulless and metallic row by an unpleasant and rough voice of a man that carried a long whip in his right fist; he appeared to be a prisoner of the past himself but he enjoyed a special rank now.

The prisoners were pulled in an inviting attempt to show them the right direction to the central stage that was specially prepared for today's occasion. Their glances were in an inseparable connection to the ground, as they climbed the stairs with their weak and weary steps. The man-keeper of the group was like a circus coach showing off his tamed set of vicious animals and his own bravery among them and their rugged teeth.

A small conclave comprised of the most powerful and influential class of the village witnessed the show, while they whispered idly to each other about their potential interests and ambitions. The grand bishop, another member of this panel, rep-resented divine aspirations in the auction. It was peculiar to see that a show of this magnitude and proportion was prepared and executed merely to please that tiny group.

The whispers of the mighty clients gained in vol-ume and some of the exchanged sentences could be heard more or less effortlessly, as they tried to convince others to bid for prisoners of obvious lower quality; soon they had forgotten their dependency on each other, as well as the respect inheriting in positions of such authority and started to argue over the potential purchases. With loud and unclear words of false wisdom they reminded each other of a proper civilized behavior and the consideration of their well deserved human rights! Each was ensured equality in the process of slave trade, which was their major source of income. The sounds of tempered clients conquered the entire atmosphere of the village and roughened the peaceful surroundings. It was the most important thing to grab the best available prisoners before the competition.

The queue of chained human products wobbled down the line like on a sushi band and their, as they were sold and handed over to the hungry members of the audience, to accept their new chains.

The Ethics of a Genocide

"Can murder be justified?" He asked himself in that very moment, as he pointed his rifle towards the nose of one of the soldiers in the enemy's uniform, who was lying silently on the muddy ground and was anxiously staring up at him. They both appeared from distance like two negligible particles in the endless fields of blood and destruction. The occasional and irregular explosive impacts were the only sources of noise. The quiet summer breeze showed its dominance and carried gently the biting fragrance of gunpowder and blood. For the first time in his life, he had the opportunity to act like a judge, a prosecutor and an executioner at the same time; this powerful position felt entirely different and more complicated than being in the trenches.

The fallen enemy was breathing heavily and his hateful face changed rapidly to a more human one that carried the signs of dreadful fear and bitter passion for survival. He had started to speak in his own language hastily; it was not clear, whether he was cursing at his enemy or simply praying for mercy. His exhausted face was not helping to decipher his words.

The imaginary court was brought to an abrupt end with a loud and unpleasant bang, which could be heard even from a long distance and seemed to add a new destructive tone to the already aggressively tempered concert of surroundings.
Later, in the beginning of a cold and apparently long lasting autumn most people didn't seem to have any difficulties to forget the brutal war. The daily life seemed to have returned, as quickly as it had left the town.

The soldier out in a dim room and without any no¯ ticeable motion stared at an empty wall. He seemed to be mesmerized by an invisible spectacle; his peaceful body was not in harmony with his restless mind. The dark memories of the past mercilessly returned and pierced his soul without any effort. It was not easy to forget the ache, the screams and the blood. The orphaned dreams and anticipations pushed him ever more into the cold and remote darkness. He could still remember the face of the slain soldier; his face was moistened by a thick mixture of his tears and cold sweat. His brightly colored blood flowed heavily and in an irregular pattern over the dusty soil in form of a small red stream that reflected joyfully the sunlight in many directions. The freshly made corpse seemed to have quietly invited a swarm of flies to another cheerful feast. The traces of the unforgettable moment were deeply carved into his soul and had replaced all memories of peace.

He tried to remember how he reached that very powerful point in his life. He could remember all the smallest details of the process of becoming a professional killer. The words, the noises and even the smells of the training were more than ever present. The unwilling return to the battle fields in his mind had become a frequent activity. Yet he kept trying to suppress all the rugged memories of the darkness.

He remembered the faces of the commanders and officers that were filled with bitterly dry hatred. They didn't seem to avoid any means to crush the invisible enemy. The luring message of fake pride was conveyed by sheer anger and intense hatred. The loud commands were supposed to cover the fact that soldiers like him were delivered to the grand beast in huge masses simply to satisfy its appetite for fresh human flesh.

He tried to find a path back to the society, although he wasn't eager to act like a social creature; the streets didn't seem to welcome their old hero anymore. People he used to trust and communicate with had become strangers, who lashed him with their lethal gazes and silent words. He felt that the entire world intended to force him into the maximum isolation.

One day as he was carrying his heavy and sorrow-
ful soul aimlessly on the streets, he suddenly
found himself in front of a cathedral of impressive
size. Although he wasn't confident of finding the
cure for his pain, he felt a strong desire to see the
majestic building also from the inside.

The major hall was lit softly and long rows of
wooden seats filled most of the space in it. Countless burning candles, which were placed in front of
a huge statue that meant to depict the sufferings
of Jesus, released nauseously divine and sacred
fumes into the great hall. The few people, who
were gathered in the holy building focused silently
on prayer and didn't seem to notice his cautious
arrival.

He suddenly realized that his steps were becoming
slower and heavier; even breathing seemed to
have become a challenge. After a few moments,
without even remembering how, he was surprised
to find himself encaged in a small wooden chamber, which appeared to be the confessional of the

cathedral. But before he had a chance to find out more, a small opening on his right side, which was crowned by a little crucifix, opened loudly; the window separated his wooden chamber from another one and was covered with a thin lattice, through which he was able to see a person, who was dressed like a priest. The priest seemed to be praying for somebody's soul and suddenly he stopped his prayer and turned towards him and said with a stertorous voice " I know you have sinned my son!" The sentence was unexpected and the words vividly brought the dark memories back again. The simple sentence unleashed a massive amount of pain and agony, violently overshadowing his perception of reality. He didn't feel he was in the confession chamber anymore, but was in the battle fields again and this time he was doomed to be merely an observer. As he was in a limbo situation between his memories and the current reality, he suddenly could see one of the furious faces of the generals on the priest's body. And that face was staring at him through the wooden grid. It was an unbearable combination of impressions. And suddenly without even noticing his actions, he pulled out a small gun from his pocket. The little pistol served him for a long period of time as a souvenir from the great war. The loud cry of three shots, which sounded like the vicious and inhuman trinity of a firing squad, awakened the entire cathedral. The priest was lying on the ground, motionless in his chamber, carrying a small hole in his head. Blood was everywhere, even in the neighboring chamber, where the shooting sinner was.

 He felt the traces of a cool thick liquid on his cheek. He tried to wipe away with the back of his left hand. He didn't notice that he was smearing the red thick liquid around his mouth; he must have looked like a blood thirsty monster. He could hear a divine melody in his mind. Although breathing was still not easy, he felt a relief in his chest. He seemed to finally grow accustomed to his expected role in the society.

Circus Maximus

The caravan was noisy and colorful and it seemed to have finally chosen a place for the next few weeks. It became slower as it was cautiously passing the narrow stony roads of the small city that was about to welcome a colorful surprise. All the bright colors and the joyful noises indicated that the show would be a success. People were eager to know what the destination of the mysterious and endless convoy was; after all it was the most exciting and maybe the most impressive event the old city has ever experienced.

Most people could sense that this commotion would be remembered for generations. The mesmerized audience followed every turn and every slight change in the acceleration of the caravan with the greatest interest. Their daily life was about to undergo an incredible and unimaginable change. The small city, where almost everything was as predictable as the sunrise and sunset, was about to witness a bashfully unforgettable event. The caravan took the longest possible way through the snaky roads of the city in a very slow tempo, as if intentionally attempting to disrupt the flow of the daily life in the town and draw more attention. Some people, who found the courage to demonstrate their curiosity, tried to approach the slowly moving caravan, in order to ask where it was heading and when they would entertain. But the desperate hunger was not yet to be satisfied; the riders of the great colorful wagons, contrary to the rest of the circus, were silent and answered the frequent questions of excitement with a simple nod towards the hills at the other side of the city.

Soon a huge tent was placed on top of the highest hill. The tent looked like a pointy crown from the distance. In the late afternoon the same crown, which managed to draw all the attention earlier, threw now its impressive a majestic shadow over a great portion of the city. The newly created darkness aroused the eagerness and curiosity of the crowd even further. From their deep and dark valley the mesmerized crowd kept staring impatiently at the breathtaking tent that was sitting quietly on the summit of the high hill. The unique and imposing entrance of the circus promised a definite continuation of entertainment in the coming days. In order to keep the excitement upright and the demands unanswered, a large area around the tent was barricaded and many visible obstacles were installed to keep the unauthorized curious away from the tent.

The next day the crowd were silently greeted by countless colorful posters, signs and flyers that had been distributed all over the city during the last night. The prayers of the people to obtain more information seemed to have been answered. The proud notice of the next show was received with passion by the majority of the population; within a few minutes the much anticipated news about the next performance was spread. This relief of the crowd after an entire day of waiting was enormous. Parents happily confirmed their eager children's attendance.

As the first night of the performance finally arrived, people marched blindly into the grand tent and were ready to be amazed. All the eye catching colors, the lustrous objects, and countless mirrors added an indescribable undertone to the already mysterious atmosphere of the circus.

The crowd, which strongly resembled well trained beasts, quietly took place in front of the stage. Their hungry eyes were about to be fed by a series of sensations; various dancers and performers welcomed the crowd acrobatically and with impressive choreography. Broad grins covered most of performers' faces with the sole intention of creating the illusion of perfect happiness. The change of performances and special effects was fast and details were difficult to follow. Colorful fumes and special illumination created an all present confusion. The performers took the breath of their audience away and keep them in an ecstatic state of constant exclamation. Every act seemed to be challenged by its previous one and hence tried to exceed the growing excitement. Above the performers a few brave souls walked over a rope that spanned gloriously from one side of the tent to other and contributed to the general amusement. Then animal handlers with their beasts climbed the stage and showed their skills and courage with the tamed predators. Some of the crowd that was sitting comfortably in the dark hall pointed at various performers and without saying a word showed their admiration and wonder and drew the attention of their neighbors to a specific part of the show.

In the midst of this commotion suddenly a tall person, who was dressed formally in a black suit, appeared. It seemed that he played a respectable role in the entire circus and his presence silently encouraged all the other performers to interrupt their act as quickly as possible and leave the entire stage to him. After a brief pause to make sure that all the other performers and animals had left, the man in black started to show some magic tricks; pulling out different objects out of his hat and various card tricks. He soon stopped and asked for a volunteer from the audience and pointed at a person and invited him to enter the stage, to which the man replied with an eager and sudden jump, appreciating his unique opportunity to be a part of this breathtaking show. He waved happily to the audience and boastfully enjoyed the special moment.

The magician then politely asked the man to enter an empty box that resembled an antique cupboard and closed its doors quickly. With firm and proud steps the magician walked across the stage, as if trying to demonstrate his unquestionable dominance of his audience. He then returned to the old cupboard and swung its doors open again. The man that entered the box just seconds ago had vanished without any visible trace. The crowd showed its surprised amusement with a loud applause.

After the disappearance of the volunteer, the magician continued with some other impressive tricks and the will-less crowd continued their hypnotized cheering.

And then suddenly the stage was swallowed by absolute and impenetrable darkness. The audience, which was disappointed by the unexpected pause, impatiently awaited the continuation of the mesmerizing show. Soon some in the audience started to express their disappointment with loud and chaotic chants, demanding the show to be carried on instantly.

But before this disappointment could be replaced by stubborn anger, a small bright circle in the middle of the stage became visible and instantly drew all attention. A person dressed in colorful puffy cloths and with a bright red wig in the center of the illuminated circle. His head hung down and he seemed to stare at his own feet. He kept his hands behind his back, as if trying to hide something from his audience.

The joyfully decorated appearance of the main character brought the people to silence again. Some even started to laugh, although there was nothing funny yet to observe, glad to realize that the show was finally about to continue.

The man in the circle of light had become the sudden center of all attention. He slowly raised his head. A mysterious wide grin covered most of his face. The thick layer of his white makeup made the smile stand out in an evil fashion. The audience followed his slight moves with blind eagerness. "Oh look, it's a clown!", shouted a person from the comfortable darkness, he and others inhabited; to this conformation of the obvious the crowd answered with a unified hoot. The clown turned his head slowly about and observed the expectant assembly once more very thoroughly. He then closed his eyes and started to sniff around. His smile was becoming more stable and confident and soon it even emitted a dominating and mighty laughter. He broke his silence suddenly with a screeching voice:" I sense my favorite fragrance again. The beautiful stench of rotten brains! It is the most pleasant perfume, the odor of stagnated souls!" After he finished this sentence, the wide smile returned to his white face. But now the smile had a more innocent and compassionate character towards the audience.

The great grand clown then slowly moved his left arm to reveal his secret. He was holding in his hand a detached human head, with the features that strongly resembled the volunteer, who had disappeared. The crowd cheerfully greeted the partial return of one their old friend. They seemed to be sure it was merely a trick. To increase the effect, after a brief pause the clown moved his other hand closer to the spectators as well. In it was a long sword that still had traces of thick fresh blood on it. In that moment the clown bowed like an indestructible hero his arms spread out to the sides.

The clown held up the head high and demonstrated once again his absolute superiority over the
crowd by swinging the head gently to every direction. The head carried the face of a surprised person; the eyes seemed to stare at the hand of the
clown and the mouth still wide open, as if trying
to scream silently. Thick drops of dark red blood
dripped off the neck slowly and splattered onto
those in the front rows. The audience were realizing this could be the highlight of the night. They
showed their unexpected pleasure with a loud
roar.

The clown took a serious posture and silently encouraged the crowd to stop the noise. He then
threw the head towards the audience and rested
the mighty sword over his right shoulder. "Go
ahead take it, you vultures! The cadaver belongs
all to you." The sensation is complete. I invite you
all to this cultural feast. Enjoy, filthy illiterate
fools!"

The Dancing Ravens

The early autumn sun seemed to have silently conquered a great portion of the center of the pale sky as if trying to convince the world of its still burning power. But the gently whispering winds had a stronger credibility and dominance over the entire nature.

The dusty village was placed between two conical hills that gave it an intimate and hidden character, and it would be difficult to know about its existence on one's first trip there. Silence flowed unnoticeably through the lifeless air and seemed to pierce the entire village. Life seemed to have reached the state of still stand and the hope of bringing it to swinging vanished softly.

In one of the most comfortable corners of the village, where the sunshine seemed to be always purer and more caring, the church was standing proudly with its tall watchtower over the rest of the village. Inside one of the major halls of the church, the priest, a tall slender person with juvenile dark hair, kept himself busy by taking an opulent oven roasted turkey apart with his bare hands. This activity seemed to demand the greatest portion of his attention. A giant bird, which seemed to have become glossier and emit colourful lights of happiness into the sacred hall, covered most of the table. Thick layers of brown and greasy joy conquered the priest's hands and mouth. A perfect moment of a joyful existence! But the meal was suddenly interrupted by loud cries from outside. The priest gently stretched his neck, still seated comfortably at the dinner table. He glanced with angry face over the cheerful table, as if trying to punish the invisible source of the annoying noise with his silent anger. Although he didn't seem to be very interested in the reason of the sudden loud noise, he knew he had to keep his professional appearance upright, so he wiped the traces of the festive meal off his face, and grabbing quickly his work tools, a pocket bible and a small wooden cross, he rushed to the wooden entrance doors of the church. Before the first step outside his holy house, he prepared himself one more time and tried to capture a worried and loving look, as if he had a feeling what he might expect behind those heavy doors.

Long rows of returning injured soldiers accompanied by other exhausted soldiers that were still able to walk, all unified by their filthy faces and clothes, were gathered in the central marketplace of the village, a great helpless mass of them expecting to be handed over to their new masters. The long silent row of the returning soldiers was greeted by surprised joy and long yearned reunion; however the screams sounded very similar. The villagers tried to approach the injured line cautiously to find out whether they could recognize a face within the dusty mass. The return of the missing, changed the entire atmosphere of the village in an unexpected fashion; everybody seemed to be challenged to remember their memories of the old days.

The priest, who also finally arrived at the market, tried to convince people to calm down, but in his mind he was still with his beloved turkey, which would soon get cold and unappetizing!

Swarms of people kept rushing to different corners of the market, where the newly arrived injured were kept, hoping to find any of their long lost relatives. The small village suddenly became more chaotic and apocalyptic than ever, as great human masses desperately searched for a familiar face or name. Every smallest possible details that would improve the state of the unknown seemed to have an immense impact like a fresh breeze of hope and encouragement to the exhausted souls. Most of the faces were soon covered with desperate tears but the search had to continue. Many people, who lost their voice after a long period of screaming the names of their beloved, were still trying to be heard in the loud human cloud, so they could tell their countless stories.

In the midst of the excited village, the priest that easily stood out of the aimless and confused crowd used the unique opportunity to be at the center of attention again. The strong smell of desperate confusion that filled the entire market was irresistible and he knew he could delightfully sell his blessings and disperse his preaching. A dream season started with the waves of misery!

Saint Sayyaf

It was one of the hottest days in the summer. The city placed in the middle of a dusty desert. People gathered to witness another spectacle that was in the public agenda. The central square of the city was prepared in a unique fashion. The numerous members of the national security guard tried to make a large human circle around the small altar in the middle of the square, preventing the entrance of the people. People eagerly tried to get a place in the front row, so they could see most of the show. The crowd was excited, but suspiciously silent. Almost everybody from the town was there; schools and all the public facilities, even the grand market, were closed. The day started like an important holiday that was not supposed to be missed.

The attendants held their breath as a small cart stopped steps away from the square and two of the guards opened the back door of it. The cart was on an important delivery mission and the crowd knew what they would receive.

A tiny old man stepped out of the cart, trying to move the heavy and rusty chains that were put all over his weak and hopeless body. His torn dirty robes made him stand out in the crowd in a peculiar way. His face was covered with injuries of different depth and age. His white beard, reaching his bare chest, covered a portion of its boney surface. His steps were unstable and exhausted.

His exit from the cart did not excite the spectators; one of the guards introduced him to the crowd and said with an unpleasant voice "This man wrote poems to ridicule our prophet! Poems everybody, poems! He is an enemy of god the almighty and today we will punish him." The cries of rage and anger filled the entire air surrounding the great square, as if this short speech ignited the passionate wrath of the masses and commanded them a demonstration of their hatred. The crowd started to throw rotten objects at the old man to show their despise towards him. But the old man did not show any reaction. He stretched his neck and looked up, as if enjoying to see the sunshine one more time.

The guard dragged him to the small altar in the center and forced him to kneel and place his wrinkly neck on the altar. The show was about to begin. The old man felt he was in the midst of blurry images and unrecognizable noises. His dry lips moved but his voice was buried under a mountain of sorrow and pain.

Soon a larger second cart, carried by two strong horses, approached the square. The dust cloud surrounding the cart promised an exciting continuation of the show. People cleared the way to make sure the cart's arrival was not disturbed. It seemed that the second cart was carrying the actual highlight of the day. Before the doors of the cart opened and revealed the real hero of the evening to the crowd, some members of the audience bowed as a sign of fearful respect. The cart made a few powerful turns around the square, before it made its way through the crowd and passed the human circle and came to a complete stop inside the square near the altar.

A tall and muscular man in a long white garment stepped down of the cart with an explosive jump, carrying a long and wide sword, almost reaching the dusty and hot ground. His face was covered with a long and untrimmed beard that displayed power and ruthlessness. His anger defined every slight move of his body and every wrinkle in his face.

Soon the process of human sacrifice could be com‾pleted; the crowd was hopeful to please their god.

The reflection of the sunlight made the tip of the long sword look like a small star that shone for a brief period of time above the human circle.

The silence shattered suddenly by a fearful cry of joy. Rays of fresh blood stained the hero's garment and part of his face. Later the hero made a few rounds in the square and encouraged people to cheer for him.

The people in the desert paradise were always far away from stability and peace; and as the moving sand they lived upon, the daily life was different day by day. Change seemed to be the only constant. Even their god didn't appreciate the vast number of their sacrifices. The powerful rulers of the country were no exception to this rule of change.

After a few weeks, city's famous hero was invited to the royal palace, this time however without his mighty sword. The new king, a small giant, observed him thoroughly with a piercing glance for a few moments, before he gave the confused hero a sign to approach him. Fear and excitement in a unique medley defined all the movements and words in the room.

The new leader with an invidious smile and a drilling tone said :" I hear people have a great deal of respect for you. It is a shame though that you worked for the previous leader." The hero remained silent and stared down at the floor, as if his old powers of confidence were all exhausted and even a direct eye contact had become a great challenge. The king then continued and said with a more intense voice:" I want to make you a generous offer. How about a similar position and services, but this time for me. And people will still fear and respect you."

The Sunday morning started with the loud cry of the bells. The newly elected bishop prepared himself for his ceremony, as he looked into the mirror that reflected a well fed man in red garment. He had to make sure that the stains of the past are not visible anymore. It was time to mesmerize the people again.

The Reign of Darkness

Mankind seems to be determined to remain obedient and accept its blunt existence under the crushing yoke of systems and institutions that dictate all the possible details of their life. Are the loudly barking men truly the powerful? It is not very pleasant to observe how throughout history human logic has been pushed away by the almighty routine. Human life seems to have been reduced to a meaningless set of rules. The great majority are willing to absorb all of the nonsense blindly and without showing any eagerness to mentally intercept and actively question them and their authority.

The morning started with a loud and strong wind that seemed to penetrate through the windows easily and spread its cold wings over his face. He had a feeling that he wouldn't make it on time today. The small garden that was fully covered with fresh white snow of the last night, warned him silently about the nature of his journey. The feeling of commitment was very strong and dominant and even the warmth of the bed was not satisfactory or convincing enough.

He was greeted silently by a mixture of snow and frozen mud that seemed to cover the entire visible horizon. The crushing snow underneath his feet made his determined steps sound rough and militaristic. The cold howling wind whipped his face and his barely covered fingers, which he used to hold his coat as close as possible to his shivering body. The heavy load of obligation made his steps slow and predictable. He felt to be mentally prepared to finish the journey, although the icy roads seemed to be endless and untameable. The lustrous white powder crowned the emptiness and made him appear like a tiny creature that was battling its way through it to a well-defined destination.

Peaceful seeming memories of the past encouraged him softly to move on and to ignore the piercing cold. After all it was going to become an important day at the church and most people he knew would be gathered there. The long and lonely walk through the frozen paradise gave him enough time to think and review some of his memories.

The silver cross, which he has been wearing as long as he could remember, seemed to give him passionately many freezing kisses, as if trying to remind him that god's love is defined by a never ending passage through agony and suffering. He always wondered why the almighty loving father ignores the pains and needs of his children, although they shouldn't be punished for the "sins" of others. People were born into various forms of misery on one side of the world, while on the other side the sun always seems to shine passionately. But maybe it was beyond his comprehension to understand the ruling methods of the almighty or maybe he simply misunderstood the definition of divine justice! He tried to convince himself and to reassign a caring image to god and hoped that his attempts of recreating god's familiar caring and powerful reputation would not end in a disappointment. He wished that his reason simply fooled him and there was more to expect from life. All his old beliefs that shaped his life thus far seemed to fade away in the painful shadows of his doubt. Suddenly he felt that the unshakeable beliefs of the past were becoming like illusive dreams and unachievable mirages.

As he finally was close enough to the church, so that he could see the sacred building through the white snow storm, he felt that the passion to enter the church and start praying was vanishing softly and was not as imperative as before. He felt a strong desire to finish the journey, in order to be obedient to his old principles, but an even stronger feeling that has been silently developing seemed to stop him from taking the next step. His steps became smaller and heavier every moment. He suddenly felt, as if he was fixed to the ground by an unknown force. Finally he stood still just a few steps away from his destination and stared at the building that seemed to have torn the snow carpet in a peculiar way to reach the sky above it. His misty breath must make him look like a rusty steaming locomotive from the distance, carrying a suddenly paralyzed soul. The moment of frozen mesmerization was then brought to an end, as he turned his head back, as if trying to review his journey from his warm bed to the current position. It was time to make a final decision, which didn't seem to challenge him in any way. After a brief moment with a determined smile he seemed to be ready to execute the fresh decision. He held his cross, which was still hanging with its cold soul on the heavy chain around his neck, one more time in his fist and stared at it, as if expecting an answer from it.

Soon an empty, deep and cross shaped mark in the snow reminded the world of his unfinished journey.

The Reflections of a Judgment

He woke up into a rough and empty darkness. He tried to squeeze his eyes to the smallest possi‑ ble source of light around himself. But the darkness was pure and impenetrable and made hope a utopian phantasy. The only thing to sense was a strange rotten smell that seemed to dominate the entire atmosphere. He took a deep breath and tried to recognize the stench. Although the strong odor was not pleasant, it might have carried pieces of lost memory or some hints about his current location, so it seemed to be important to identify it.

As he continued to look aimlessly to find more about the nature of his dark surrounding, the sound of a striking match at the other end of the room took the silent darkness apart. In the light of newly burnt matchstick, a small portion of somebody's hand became visible, which was trying to bring a half burnt cigar to a revived smoulder. After a brief pause, a small light, which seemed to be placed on a table in front of him, was turned on and released its brightly annoying rays towards his tired face. A husky voice, whose owner seemed to be behind the source of light, said without any relevant introduction:" I'll be your judge, your prosecutor and ..." For a moment the voice came to a sudden short pause; the owner of the mysterious voice leaned then forward gently, so part of his poorly shaved chin could be seen in the bright cone of light and then continued ", and your executioner, if necessary!"

He felt a strong desire to ask the self-proclaimed judge questions about his status quo, but he was not able to talk. The heavy words seemed to be dammed behind his lips. His disability to release those heavy words was more irritating than being kept in darkness in front of the apparently mighty judge. He was convinced that he could break the boundaries only with an impossibly loud and powerful scream.

Instead he found himself climbing a filthy and empty spiral staircase, which didn't seem to lead to anywhere specific. He had the impression to be pulled up by an unknown force, as if he was obligated to be up there. The darkness seemed to follow each of his steps.

He then heard a desperate and helpless voice that cried for help. It was a familiar voice, although he couldn't recall whose voice it was and how he would know it. The intensity of feelings didn't let his feet rest. Now it was more than the mere curiosity that encouraged his climbing; reaching the top seemed to have become a human responsibility of highest priority. The challenge of endless seeming stairs numbed his legs, but he knew he couldn't give up the battle and the journey had to come to an end soon.

Often it was small things that would be barely noticeable, which forced him to return to the dark room. His senses were unnecessarily sharp and didn't seem to allow his exhausted soul rest. Although it was difficult to distinguish between the darkness in his dreams and the real dark, he preferred the one in his dreams; satisfying his curiosity about the source of the cries seemed to have become more important than his own destiny.

As he opened his eyes again, the darkness was still there and it seemed to have become bitterly more intense.

"Applause, applause! The hamster is back in its wheel!" said the judge with a biting sarcasm, as if trying to remind him of another wasted day of his existence.

The dream seemed to return with ever stronger emotions; a clash of needs and agitations. The cries of the unknown seemed to get more intense and incredibly less human every time. He felt he was approaching the main source of agony and was about to find out more about it. The stairs were becoming narrower and filthier step by step. The bestial squeaking sounds of the helpless unknown were becoming more disturbing. He was almost out of breath, as he finally reached the top of the staircase and stepped onto an empty platform that was barely lit. His energy was fading and his legs almost failed to carry his exhausted soul; with a broken breath he tried to locate the place of the whipping sounds of the unknown. He then carefully approached the farthest cliff of the platform, where the sounds of sorrow, which rather resembled noises of a small and worthless rodent from this short distance. He suddenly realized a set of shivering fingers that were passionately clinging on the filthy edge of the platform, as if uniformly trying to ensure the survival of their master. He felt a strong curiosity to see the face of the unknown, before even saving him. He bent cautiously over the edge to be able to see more of the owner of those desperate fingers. His head hung down, as if mesmerized by the breathtaking view. The living noises from the top of the platform however encouraged him to slowly raise his head and look up. The moment that he would see the face of the unknown, whose voice he has been following him for the last few days, even when he wasn't asleep,

117

was filled with fearful anticipation accompanied by heavily choking silence. But before the face of the unknown was entirely recognizable, the dream was shattered by bright lights that illuminated the entire room for the first time since his arrival. He had suddenly a childish desire to be able to return to the dream one more time to try to help the unknown or at least identify him. He kept his eyes closed, not only to avoid the bright light, which has turned to an alien creature, but also to be able to review the last portions of his dream. It was an attempt to recognize at least parts of the dream and associate them with people he knew. He forced himself to imagine a plausible ending to the chain of his dreams.

His eyes were finally accustomed to the penetrating bright light, as he realized the slow approach of the judge, whose face was covered with dried tears, as if he was suddenly able to take pity on his helpless convict. The face, which became visible for the first time, seemed to be peculiarly familiar, as if it was the one he used to see every day. He seemed to be mesmerized by recognizing the face of the judge. The judge then took a deep breath and stared passionately at him before starting to talk again. He anticipated anxiously the judge's next words, although he had an impression to sense the outcome. "The judge has found you guilty!" said the judge with a shaky voice.

He nodded silently and repeated with a sigh:" guilty, guilty..!" At that moment he could imagine the last image of the unknown person from his dreams. That face could be easily replaced by judge's misery hit face. It was the same misery he was familiar with from his daily glance at mirror. He kept repeating tearfully the verdict until releasing his clinging fingers off the top of the platform and disappearing into the heart of darkness.

The Lost Prayer

The fall was about to end and everything started to become more strange. The leaves, the wind even the rain seemed to intend to change everything. People prepared themselves to complain about the cold, as if pain they had to suffer would be the sudden cold.

The cry of black crows filled the cold air and gave the small garden a mysterious and eerie undertone. The garden had lost its initial vivid image and seemed to be aging faster than before. The piles of colorful leaves, separated carefully from the rest of the muddy garden, seemed to guard the walls.

His mind was busy again. He was trying to organize his thoughts, while he kept himself occupied by collecting the rest of the leaves that had fallen on the ground again. "It is going to be another early winter" he thought, although he knew that was not his major concern.

He remembered silently his old dream again,

which motivated him to make the move and to dedicate his entire life. He still could remember clearly that dream, which shaped his life since then. Maybe everything else was still part of the same dream. He wondered.

The sudden loud scream of the church bell shattered his annoying daydream and warned him about the upcoming ceremony that was not to be missed. He gratefully forced himself towards the cathedral and decided to prepare himself for the divine service and to follow god's will once again. As he carefully entered the main hall, all the other brothers were already deep in prayers. They seemed to be waiting patiently for the blessed entrance of the bishop. He noticed the noise his shoes produced seemed to have bothered some of the focused audience, so he quietly tried to find a place to sit and pretended to know the exact page of the prayers book, from which a song of appreciation and gratitude towards the merciful god was chosen to celebrate his holiness's presence.

As the bishop started to talk about a familiar parable from the bible, he was somewhere else in his mind. He still felt that he was carrying the dilemma of the unfinished work in the garden in his mind. He was hoping that the wind hadn't destroyed his earlier efforts already. He tried to avoid remembering the dream, which used to make him feel very unique and special; he would tell everybody about the dream in any given occasion like an old officer that would show off proudly his entire set of medals. But now the same dream seemed to have become a source of annoyance and not of honor anymore.

The monk that was sitting next to him put a sudden end to his reviving dream as he indicated to him with an easily recognizable wide smile how delighted and lucky he felt that the grand bishop honored their monastery with his visit. He responded to the brother with a slow and silent nod, without even understanding the passionate anecdote. Although he understood the innocent joy of the monk, he was not able to imitate it.

His return to the small garden was welcomed by a yellow carpet of leaves that seemed to be trying to hide the mud from him. He was glad to see the garden's loyalty towards him, always seeming to prod him with reasons to get busy, although he pretended to be bothered by the amount of work he was exposed to.

Sometimes he wished he was able to turn the time back; just once more being able to have that dream and having the possibility to think about it more thoroughly. But he knew the wish was not realistic and in addition to that he couldn't simply give up the monastery after the entire cold and empty garden has developed a direct shortcut into his soul.

As he continued to collect the rest of the leaves, he wished to find an excuse to return to the old chapel with a hope of being able to discover a fresh reason to dream again, as if the garden was not able to offer a haven for his restless mind.

His only fear was that one day he would wake up and realize that he had been fooled and his life-long dedication was just an irreversible waste. The frightening possibility that the dream could come to an end stole the last peaceful moments from his mind. But he knew it was too late to regret and tried to overcome the inner struggle and convince himself about the degree of true reliability of his dream. "The Lord wouldn't let me down! He can't just be a mesmerizing nightmare!" He affirmed to himself with a fading but hopeful inner voice.

The Departed

In the distance a small boat could be seen, battling its way through the powerful see. The old fisherman was very quiet, as he had been since the beginning of this journey. His white beard bothered his clear sight. Even the boat seemed to complain constantly with a series of loud squeaks, but the fisherman was determined to end the miserable journey with his guest, a well-dressed young man that seemed to be here for the first time.

The young man pressed his thick coat together with his right hand and held his hat with the other one. Sometimes he tried to encourage the old fisherman into a conversation, upon which he always received the same answer: silence! After that the old man avoided any direct eye contact, as if he preferred to listen to the wrath of the sea. One of the first things from the small island that could be seen was a stony tower of ancient origin. Standing proudly atop a rocky cliff and narrating silently countless stories of the past.

The presence of thick clouds darkened the endless skies over the island and gave the arrival of the boat a heavy and unforgettable impression.

As he prepared himself to thank the fisherman, he realized that the silent old man was already on his way to return again. Soon the fisherman unified with the restless waves and disappeared.

Although the paradox image of chilling peace was very impressive, he decided to continue his journey. He followed then a narrow road that seemed to be the only way to penetrate into the depths of the new island.

The few stubborn tress that flanked the old road, seemed to be dancing in a windy concert. The movement of their lower branches were like hands of a curious child trying to cautiously approach the new stranger on their lonely island.

Like a floating ark above the golden waves of tall grass, the small houses started to appear on the horizon. The view gave him a peculiar elixir of contradicting emotions; he felt like a lost stranger close to home. He put his suitcases for a brief moment on the ground and took a deep breath. The streets were lifeless and the wind kept blowing through the cold emptiness. A wooden old sign of a guest house, whose letters had become indecipherable over the years, was rattling up and down in the wind. He stretched his neck to see the house in its full glory; a peaceful residence of comfort of old times.

When he entered the guest house, he was surrounded by darkness. His cautious steps on the brown wooden floor created an alarming noise and notified his arrival. A middle aged woman appeared at the other side of the room. Her face was filled with unexpected and surprising joy to see a new guest. However she tried to conceal the emotions and look more professional, as she pretended to be busy cleaning up the room and putting the chairs at their best positions next to various tables. It seemed that she was trying to encourage her new guest to use all of the furniture at once.

Without showing any intention of getting involved in a long conversation, he asked the woman about a vacant room, to which she responded with a silent but inviting hand gesture.

The small room in the attic was furnished with a bed, a chair and a tiny table. The walls carried marks of the dried moisture that decorated them with various patterns. The secretive smell of the mighty sea breeze that has been penetrating into the room was the only inhabitant of the room. He knew that the room was just his first discovery on the unusually dull island.

The next day the wind blew less violently, as if it got used to the new traveller's existence. The illusion of a perfect paradise removed all the peace from his mind and its silent invitations seemed to be irresistible. The joy of having found a unique haven where the memories of past couldn't find him and scratch his soul guided him through the unknown alleys of the island. Although the pain was still there, the hope to be able to run away from it, didn't lose its power and dragged him through the newly discovered streets of the island. He felt the power of emptiness crawling all over his exhausted soul; forgetting the past seemed to be the only cure. He didn't know what to expect, but he had to carry on.

Every step into the unknown revived many memories of the past in an incredible way. Whenever he tried to feel like a curious stranger determined to find refuge, the unfamiliar walls of the city brought him mercilessly back to his bitter reality. He had hoped to find a mental remedy, a soothing balm for his torn soul, yet even the mighty winds were not capable to wipe away the old painful dust off his mind. She was still all present in his mind and her laughters echoed in his mind. She did not disappear by his long journey into the unknown world; in his mind, she was still there with all her breathtaking beauty.

Guided by sheer curiosity, he soon entered a small stony path that led to another side of the island.

The sound of the sea could be heard from the distance and soon it was accompanied by misty howling winds. He continued his way that melted into a rocky cliff. The great eagerly welcomed his arrival with dark blue foamy waves. The grieving blue sea resembled a loving mother, separated from her son for a long time. But now she could tell him countless untold stories of the past that were buried under her blue waves.

The cold and vicious wind whipped his face and seemed to pierce his body. He could hear his own heartbeat that was becoming in harmony with the savage blue sea. The sea kept mourning and releasing its naked anger at the rocky cliff with loud and foamy waves; he felt he had become an indispensable part of this perfect symphony of sorrows. Heavy droplets of tear made silently frosty trails downwards over his cheeks, as if trying to unify him with the great blue sea. He had discovered that his destination was not far enough and his old agony had found him again.

The exhaustion flowed in all bits and pieces of his body and managed to pour out any last signs of passion and hope from him. His legs failed to carry his lonely soul. The vicious blue had become a familiar and gentle beast and the sound of its watery fists of wrath sounded like a heavenly choir of trustworthy angels. It was time to make a decision. He was far away from home but he had a feeling, this journey was about to end.

The Unforgettable Wounds

The darkness seemed to silently have de‐
cided to reside at all the corners of the room. The
pale sunlight was carefully separated from the
room by thick curtains. The windows didn't seem
to have been opened for a long time and there
didn't seem to be any reason to change their state;
the birds had stopped singing for a while and even
the air in the neighborhood seemed to have lost its
pleasant and joyful smell of the past. The voice of
an old radio from the next room softly penetrated
through the walls and spread heavy sweet tones of
better days, as if trying to distract minds from
their present agony. It was difficult to understand
and remember how the old vivid streets had sud‐
denly become a comfortable nest for pain and
grief.

He still wasn't able to taste his soup that was pre‐
pared for him earlier to comfort him. His exhaust‐
ed soul didn't seem to let him realize his hunger.

The detailed images of the last incident have quietly become like engravings, carved deeply into his soul. The tears may be dried by now, but the painful memories were determined to last longer. The waves of refugees that had to flee their houses, changed the entire character of the town, where everyday life with all of its different aspects and stages happened; the hopeful weddings, the playing children, the old friendships, the passionate dreams and all the memories were shattered in a brief glimpse. The muddy lifeless streets were now decorated with forgotten objects of the past; broken furniture, work tools and even destroyed toys.

Thinking about a tomorrow seemed to have become the hardest thing, although he remembered many other occasions, where he had to find the strength and courage to stand up again and dream of better days. But now blood and destruction had invaded the endless horizons of his capabilities. The hateful roaring of the demon of war sounded stronger, a dull thunder in the distance, but that didn't even to have its initial power to disturb him anymore. His ears were becoming immune to the bestial noises that replaced the sounds of lively hope and passion on the streets; the untameable sounds of bombings and gunshots conquering the once lively city.

The painful memories marched over his mind and trampled his passion. Even his strongest beliefs, the most powerful ideologies that had shaped his entire life and defined his mental backbone seemed now suddenly meaningless and without their previous silent comfort.

As he stared at his empty hands, he still could see the reflections of the girl's face covered with a thick layer of sorrow. Her voice still filled present in the room. The last glance at her small face with her candy apple red make up that stained her familiar but now hardly recognizable soft smile, defined the moment. He had continued screaming her name, trying to encourage her to wake up and to run around as in the old days. But his screams didn't seem to be loud enough to bring her back. With a face covered with tears of pain he raised his tired head and observed silently but filled with anger the endlessly grey sky, as if trying to show his pain to god himself and complain about his negligence.

He remembered his days when her joyful voice filled the air in the entire neighborhood and gave it playfully a vivid and hopeful identity. Her piercing voice was now replaced by the vicious cries of destruction. And now without the familiar lively voices, the city seemed to have become merely a grey collection of lost memories.

Shades of Pain

The dark and cold night seemed to be di⁻
vided into two halves, as the loudly crying train
cut through the forest quickly. It was a cold winter
that lasted already more than usual. Inside the
train was yet colder and more soulless than the
outside. Only a few people populated quietly the
long hall with countless rows of wooden benches.
He was sitting on one of the middle rows, resting
his heavy and tired head on the dusty window and
trying to ignore the biting cold wind that penetrated through the edges of the window. He was
exhausted but couldn't sleep. He still could imagine her warm face in the frozen dust that covered
the window glass. He remembered every single
word that he exchanged with her before his final
departure. He remembered how she was comfort-
ing him and making him smile. The presence of
heavy droplets of tear that making watery semi-
rings in his eyes could not be ignored. He pressed
his eyelids to prevent losing those tears, after all

it was not appropriate to weep in an almost empty train.

As he opened his eyes again, he only saw the re-flection of a tired old man in the heart of the win-dow. His silvery hair, barely covered by a hat, poked through and seemed to illuminate his face. He almost had forgotten his own appearance. He kept staring at the frozen horizon through the dusty window with the childish hope to bring her face back again, but all he saw was cold and lone-ly darkness that even the incredible speed of the train could not escape.

His gaze into the endless and pure darkness was interrupted by the cry of a child that had difficul-ties ignoring the vicious cold and continuing his sweet dreams. The painful screams spread to all the corners and pierced all the walls of the train. He lifted his head to find the source of the noise; he envied the child's courage to express his suffer-ings that freely and carelessly. At the same time he tried to conceal this great sin by looking annoyed around, as if attempting to punish the child for tearing his bitter dreams of the past apart. He silently kept staring at the child in a way to show his fake dominance and control from the distance, although he felt closer and more intimate to the mysterious child and found a missing portion of his own soul in the crying child.

The last squealing sign of life in the train faded away, as the child gave up the cry. He must have realized his loud and honest tears would not make the train or his own seat warmer.

Her innocent voice was always present in his mind and even the cold wind that caressed his skin failed to bring him back to the world of the freezing train. Old memories were still parts of his reality.

He wished he had the power to turn the head of the train in opposite direction; he imagined how eagerly he would expect the end of the journey then. He would probably stand impatiently in the front part of the train just to be a bit closer to his destination. He would jump off the train as the first person and see her again in the station. But he knew it was a naive aspiration and the journey could not be reversed. He felt deeply weak and lost.

He took a careful sip from the cup of his black coffee. The cup was placed in front of him since the beginning of his cold journey, waiting to wake him with its bitterness. The moving train shook the cup and some of it spilled on the floor; it seemed that even the frozen train insisted the dreams continued.

Next day he woke up again, as the sunlight managed to penetrate through the deep dust of the windows and gently touched his eyelids. He couldn't remember when he fell asleep and what happened since last night. The train had come to a strange stop. All passengers were still in deep sleep and didn't notice this stop. Even the child had found his peace at last.

He felt a powerful temptation to leave the train

immediately, although he was certain that the train did not reach its final destination yet; his soul was still in cold pain, and his mouth was bitter from the remnants of last night's coffee.

He observed carefully the small station to find a motivation or a sign to stand up and to end the exhausting journey. He knew that it would be very difficult at that time to find the power and courage for such an abrupt change. He hoped that the train would mercifully spare some more time and give him the chance to fulfill his ambitions. He felt he was trapped in a metallic cage of chocking loneliness.

Soon the train made an incredibly loud noise to show off its readiness to continue the infinite journey. The warning noise shook him off the dream world. His request for more time was denied!

As the train started to gain its original speed again, he found himself rushing aimlessly through the long corridors of the train. These corridors resembled endless and dark tunnels, leading to a distant and unknown place. He increased his speed without knowing where he was going, as if he was searching a beloved person at the other end of the train.

He realized he was not capable of defeating the powerful and merciless train. He collected all his power one more time to reach one of the windows in the hallway, to sniff some fresh air and continue his run. The train was passing a long bridge that connected two mountains and seemed to float above a river of deep blue. The reflection of the sunlight made the river look like a majestic residence of eternal freedom and peace and it seemed to seductively invite him as its new member.

The morning seemed to be full of new dreams, hopes and expectations. The great clock in the center of the station seemed to mesmerize its audience with one last warning to prepare themselves for their next journeys. A mixed smell of

145

fresh coffee and smoke revived the old station again and gave it an unforgettable impression of the place of happy reunions as well as painful departures. The silence before another great storm was deceiving.

The Fading Memories

The morning was cold and the heavy fog con‾
troled the empty streets. The silent early winter
tried to convince the giant trees in town to give in
and release their colorful leaves.

It was a special day for him. He was expecting this
day for a long time. A confusing excitement com-
bined with lack of eagerness, seemed to dictate
him a different perception of his surroundings. The
warning sound of the ticking old clock dominated
the air in the room, as if intending to take his cup
of coffee away. He stared at the clock angrily for a
brief moment, trying to punish it and reply to its
unnecessary warnings. He knew it was time to put
on the heavy boots and move on. A stinging weak-
ness controlled his motions and even holding the
almost empty cup felt like an overwhelming challenge. He looked around himself and tried to absorb all the possible details of the familiar room
for one more time. It seemed that the old furniture have created a special connection to his very
soul and reminded him softly of the memories of

the past. But he knew it was getting late.

A smoking metallic beast of enormous dimensions, covering a large portion of the shore, was expecting to refresh its load and to return to the endless seeming blue of the sea.

The small paths that led to the port were prepared in a very peculiar way. They were flanked by signs of different size displaying the relevance and the invisible glory of the day. The numerous loudspeakers enchanted the area nearby with passionate yet monotonous nationalistic melodies that demonstrated a unique and incredible greatness that needed unconditional attention again. The heavy and intense notes gave a serious and grey image to the harbor that has always been famous for being the most vivid section of the town.

A great human mass that was dressed in a similar way, silently welcomed him. The long roads were filled with exhausted people of different age, unified by their identical destination.

The enormous and mind blowing dimensions of

the grey beast became more and more noticeable, as he and other soldiers next to him approached it step by step. The marching journey was slow, although its end was not anticipated. The long row of the waiting soldiers was suddenly encouraged to stop for the process of unloading the wooden boxes that contained the fallen heroes from the last trip. It was important to make sure that all the boxes are taken out, so there is enough space for the new set of soldiers. A fearful silence filled the air and seemed to penetrate every soul.

He lowered his head, as if trying to pay attention to every detail of the dusty road. The moment gave him an unfamiliar combination of helplessness and desperate anger.

As the dimension and contents of the giant ship became more visible, many of the soldiers started to pray.

The mighty daemon of war had appetite for young fresh meat again and the powerful army didn't hesitate to satisfy its hunger, delivering constantly a fresh load of the desired human mass.

The strong stench of death distracted the soldiers from all the powerful and mesmerizing signs and dimmed the invisible glory of the day. Soldiers slowly reached the last point on the road, where their family and friends could accompany them.

As he turned away to join the others, he heard her voice again. He stretched his right arm and without noticing opened his fist of rage, as if trying to gently touch her with the tip of his fingers from the distance one more time. But the last silent farewell was violently interrupted by the mighty human wave that pushed him away from her. Even his firm step couldn't avoid his drowning into his destiny. His shivering weak right hand still directed towards her face, could be seen from the distance as a last sign of his resistance. He became slowly an unnoticeable droplet within enormous waves of dismay.

The soldiers, unified in their looks and agony, walked slowly over the small bridge that was the last connection between the metal giant and the harbor. Their exhausted souls were not able to carry their heavy heads. They all were silent in their glorious death row!

The young soldiers were taken to a small chamber that polished their faces and washed away their individuality. The war required faceless fresh meat and this was the first step to ensure the desired quality of the products that were about to be delivered. Soulless small plaques that carried engraved numbers of militaristic identification were distributed to show the soldiers the importance of their future return as fallen heroes.

The steel slave ship fully loaded with its precious blinded human flesh, started its journey, crushing the wavy wrath of the mighty blue sea, headed irreversibly towards its destination to please its god of war.

The Tamed Souls

Dark layers of cloud crowned the concrete building that stood there with a silent pride and resembled impenetrable militaristic forts. Atop the dead moor the proud prison challenged the apparent eternity of the flat lands.

The hour of noon encouraged all the existing souls to refrain from their mandatory jobs, in order to have a brief break, before returning to their assigned positions, as was expected by the society.

Soon a grey mass of dazed and uniformed people filled the exterior yard, as if somebody had suddenly opened their small cages and given them the impression of a momentary freedom. Their exhausted faces were all blackened by a makeup of dark grease. As the grey human cloud slowly left the concrete prison, even the weakest ray of sunlight was able to irritate their hungry eyes. The fact that their spirits still had to carry heavy chains of misery didn't seem to bother them. Mesmerized by a piercing illusion, everyone rushed around aimlessly and tried to find the best empty spot in the yard. A huge clock, which was placed in such a way that made it easily visible from every corner, warned silently about the approaching end of the beloved break. The governing silence gave then a sudden birth to a chaotic human concert. The crowd was blinded by thick layers of darkness that dictated monotonously every aspect of their meaningless existence.

The grey assembly, which gradually started to get used to the demanding light, was guarded by a few armed persons in darker uniforms. The guards confidently showed their eagerness to crush any slightest desire to breathe free. But the heavy and overwhelming routine has already managed to eradicate any source of individual creativity. Even the words that were exchanged didn't represent anything new and were merely the usual and harmless complaints, and nothing else. They all seemed to have accepted that they were placed in an invisible closed circle and were not allowed to exit it, ever!

The impaling glances of the guards remained barely noticeable, as the participants of the holy break were busy with their food. Their bellies easily governed their minds.

A heavy and suffocating smell dominated the air in the yard and choked innocent smiles on every face.

The silent invitation of the great clock to count the minutes to the end of the break was passionately accepted by everybody, as if they could use the break to hide their deeper and more intense desire to return to the darkness. The temptation to reach the comfortable lap of the almighty routine was irresistible again!

As the large clock finally showed the official end of the break, the guards, who had anticipated this moment for a while, became uniformly alarmed. Their movements were sudden and unpredictable. They used their loud and high pitched whistles to encourage the grey mass to return to their work. People followed eagerly the whistles and hastily built a fairly ordered line; they resembled a will-less flock of well-behaved sheep forced to trust their loud shepherds, who took the responsibility to bring the precious sheep safely back to work. The grey buildings, which everybody escaped just minutes ago, suddenly seemed to have become the safest shelter to protect the helpless people from the invisible wolves of freedom.

Every step was predetermined and the good sheep pushed themselves and guided each other to the right direction through the dark and narrow tunnels to their initial positions. The existence of the guards was becoming more obsolete day by day, as the shadows of obedience overpowered the skies of logic. The building's interior was the place, where all these good and will-less citizens gathered. A short lived chaos greeted the newly arrived mass and made itself noticeable to all of their senses. But the gathering was to end soon; the returned mass divided itself voluntarily into different streams, in order to reach their designated destination the fastest possible way.

The main hall was a dim place that embodied countless working stations; these stations were simply called the boxes and were separated from each other by thin sheets of a rough material. Each box had the necessary number of tools, nuts, screws and other well-greased instruments. Everybody seemed to know exactly what was expected. Nevertheless almost all the walls were covered with different signs or notes, which carried various instructions and regulations. There were also some other signs that simply tried to define an ideal worker. These signs of unnecessary encouragement were accompanied by some loud messages of a hawkish nature that found their way through the huge loudspeakers to the unarmed ears of the silent people. The timbals of the masters had to be heard clearly and without any possible interruption; the speakers and the signs, which carried these vital messages, hence enjoyed the greatest attention and maintenance in the entire building.

There were no windows in the entire building. The scent of recycled air was forced through the halls by many huge fans and air channels that were placed in multiple positions to produce an imitation of freshness. The procedure of the work was monotonous and the workers appeared like pre-programmed toys that performed silently repetitive motions in exactly the same order to please their masters. From the distance the image resembled a mechanical orchestra; each motion was strictly defined and any move that didn't match the predefined rules was considered a great sin and was meant to be avoided. The early and dominant presence of the guards and the silent signs were very effective, as the practice of forbidden motions and thoughts were erased from the behavior of the people. The sense of curiosity has been easily replaced by the will of the authority.

In the minds of the naive workers disobedience has always been set equal to blasphemy. A so-called good worker was characterized by his blind and absolutely unshakeable compliance with the rules of productivity. Disobedience and individuality were meant to be avoided and fought in its basic and early stages, so the potential opportunity of an irregularity wouldn't even be created.

The dark surrounding was meant to discourage the working mass from talking, but sometimes they were not able to resist the involuntary involvement in random short conversations. It was not impossible to overhear the hopes, wishes and fears that dominated these talks. "Do you know what keeps me motivated?" Said a worker to one of his comrades. A heavy grin, which would freeze immediately as soon as he ended the first sentence, accompanied his shaky voice. "The possibility that one day I will work in a larger box with more tools!" He then answered his own earlier question in a softer tone and continued his work with even more attention than before, as if trying to conceal his revived inner agony.

The work gave everybody an opportunity to cling

passionately from the precious cliff of existence that could be easily defined within the over-whelming grey walls; an existence that had only one apparent purpose: reaching the absolute and unchallengeable state of stagnation! The blunt and monotonous existence within the grey walls of the factory was the only thing imaginable to the crowd and they were neither able nor ready to compre-hend being beyond those walls.

Caught in the mighty claws of monotony, which dictated them every heartbeat, every thought and every move; days passed, the work continued and the masses were bombarded by repetitious heavy messages that were conveyed by the giant speak-ers. There was no rest for the mighty trumpets of the establishment; the powerful words were ac-companied by the jingle of the metallic tools and the occasional hammering. A mechanical and mo-notonous concert swallowed all the other human sounds like a starving demon from a distant world. In the midst of the almighty concert, the speakers suddenly stopped; the absolute unimaginable was about to happen. It took a while for the workers to realize the sudden failure. Soon silence dominated the entire atmosphere and gave the giant hall a serious and heavy character. The crowd stopped their work for the first time outside the regular break time. They all slowly raised their necks and stared at the speaker that was closest to their box. Wonder and disbelief seemed to have con-quered all the faces at once. Even the guards, who had of course been prepared for any unexpected situation, came to a sudden freeze as well, as if the speakers were the engines of their motivation to continue.

Careful listeners were soon able to detect some soft alien noises. The workers and guards were gazing at each other in speechless wonder, maybe with the desperate hope of finding some signs of comfort in somebody else's exhausted and greasy face.

The silence was shattered again, as the speakers

with an increasing volume started to work again; but for the first time they were spreading tones of a different nature; neither the usual motivating messages, nor the simple descriptions of an ideal worker. It sounded more like music, Vivaldi's summer to be more accurate! A powerful and impressive piece of music that would easily stick in the memory. The penetrating cry of the violins meant to create a new hope of resurrecting revolution seemed to have a divine connection. After years of listening to the piercing speeches, it was hard to believe that the speakers were capable of producing such unfamiliar gentle tones. After a few moments the music gained enough power, so it would flow to the even most remote corners of the main hall of the factory. The global state of astonishment reached its climax. The mesmerized crowd continued their fixed gazes at the speakers, as if the source of the music was visible through the giant horns. The guards were the first to regain consciousness and immediately with their loud whistles attempted to encourage the workers to release themselves from the overwhelming joy and return to work without causing any further trouble. As this noisy request remained unattended and the workers without noticing refused to continue their work, the guards started to beat some of the workers that were closest to them with their sticks, not only to distract their attention away from the speakers, which suddenly have become the objects of hatred, but also to show their ability and readiness to punish rebellious workers when necessary. The loud and irritating screams were buried under the heavy music, as the rest of the working crowd quietly observed the bloody spectacle.

The rest of the assembly resembled a collection of tamed animals waiting to be slaughtered by their loving masters! They seemed to have forgotten every sign, by which they would be considered human; even the most trivial skill to scream out their deep agony could not be recalled. They had grown accustomed to the invisible chains of their work and had become indispensable parts of the great grey factory. Many even appreciated the efforts of the guards that were fighting against the frightening chaos to save the spirit of the day. With their silence they showed their approval and the deeper wish to be able to overcome the mess and continue their work. The newborn chaos changed the entire atmosphere rapidly in an unfamiliar way and eliminated the old certainty.

Few, if any, realized that replacing the messages of productivity by a powerful piece of music would have such an impressive impact on the powerful routine and bring the whole factory to a collapse. Nobody showed any desire to find out what might be the reason for this tumult; a technical defect, a childish prank, an experiment or all of this simply the product of the imagination of an undetected worker.
The chaos lasted a few more minutes until all speakers were turned off. But the previous state

of productivity would not be reached immediately. The working crowd had yet to wait briefly before they were able to return safely to the almighty arms of the trusted order and to uniformly continue the work. The next precious break didn't seem to be far away!

Printed in Great Britain
by Amazon